I0764650

Flight of the Great Blue Heron

Flight of the Great Blue Heron

Rachel Secor

Brightleaf Press

Brightleaf Press
Jacksonville, Florida

Cover art by Savannah Seaver

ISBN: 978-1-939098-06-1 (hardcover)
ISBN: 978-1-939098-07-8 (paperback)
ISBN: 978-1-939098-08-5 (e-book)

Printed in the United States of America.

First Edition

Chapter One

Sam was all alone with his discovery. For the first time since moving to the country, Sam Hobbs wished that he had someone his own age to talk to, someone to share his treasures with. He and his mother had moved from Mount Marcus to his grandfather's farm in Ivers, some thirty miles to the north, at the beginning of summer. He hadn't met any kids to play with yet, and so he felt lonely. Only the excitement of exploring his grandfather's farm kept his mind occupied. During the day, Sam's mother worked as a freelance writer at a desk in their den. Sam knew to be quiet and to stay out of her hair whenever she sat at the desk with her back to the door. He hardly saw his grandfather, Otis J. Hobbs, because of all the odd jobs people hired him to do in town. So Sam was all alone with his discovery.

Sam entered the house knowing that his mother still worked in the den, even though it was close to bed time. He flew up the stairs and into the bathroom to fill the sink with water. He got a better look at his new treasure under the overhead lights. Dirt had caked thick on it like cement, covering a flat disk and rough handle. What a find! He knew that he'd uncover something of value if he kept digging in the old barn long enough. Dunking it into the water, Sam scrubbed it with his toothbrush until he could identify it. Never before had he seen a magnifying glass this large. It covered his two hands put together. Pleased that it didn't look like an ordinary magnifying glass, he dried and polished it with a towel. The light-pink glass measured at least a half-inch thick, almost as thick as the dark wood that framed it. It looked like an over-sized watermelon lollipop. Sam examined the deep-cut squiggly lines around the frame and down the sides of the handle. In the center of the top frame, entwined in a vine-like scroll, he could make out two sprawling initials, "P.W."

A chill came over Sam as he studied the letters. Who was P.W.? Moving into his bedroom, he concluded that P.W. must have been one of the men who had helped build the old barn. Whoever P.W. had been, Sam was glad that he had left his magnifying glass in the barn. It had to be the best find of the summer, a real treasure.

As he looked through the pink lens, everything became huge, and he could see the smallest detail. Sam moved around his room, viewing everything through the lens. He even studied the fibers of his carpet and saw beachball-sized hunks of lint and rock-sized grains of dirt trapped between its columns. With a yank, he then pulled out a shaft of his own dark hair. The whitish bulb at its end resembled the bulb of a green onion that grew in the garden. Even the curves and ruts of his fingertips looked like a fascinating maze of swirls and gullies. He jumped onto the bed and looked at the blue hairy back of a lifeless fly in the corner of the window sill.

From the fly, he turned his attention to the window screen. As he looked past the now enlarged aluminum squares of the screen, the stone wall that separated his grandpa's land from a large hay field came into focus. Like the evening before, a low, rolling mist moved over it. In the twilight-greyness, the mist looked like great puffy swirls of cotton-candy resting on the stubbles of hay. Mesmerized by the mist and the coming darkness, Sam couldn't take his eyes away from the glass. Suddenly, as if in a movie, a stagecoach pulled by four black horses raced into view. The coach veered around a huge solitary oak near the road, not far from Sam's window. The large white letters of TITUS STAGE LINES covered the coach door panel. Suddenly, a man's face appeared in the window of the coach. Sam watched in amazement as the man leaned out and stared directly at him.

"Oh my gosh!" Sam gasped as he dropped the magnifying glass. He sat for a moment and rubbed his eyes. When he looked out the window again, he saw nothing but the misty field. With trembling hands, he picked up the magnifying glass and slowly brought it back in front of his face. But this time he saw only the large squares of the screen. Not even the hay field could be seen in the darkness.

Early the next morning after breakfast, Sam jumped the stone wall and ran toward the old oak tree in the field. As he made his way through the dewy knee-deep grass, he almost tripped over a huge snapping turtle. It had to be at least a foot and a half long from head to tail. Any other time he would have been excited to see such a creature, and he would have spent the whole day watching it. But not this day. He had more important things on his mind. He had a mystery to solve.

A rush of screaming crows filled the air. Sam stopped for a moment to watch their chaotic flight, and then he turned his attention to the stream that snaked along the property line. A great blue heron swiftly took flight from the stream's muddy bank and swooped over his head. As he watched the large bird's graceful form, Sam felt a connection with the lone bird. He closed his brown eyes and imagined himself soaring through the air alongside the heron.

The persistent buzzing of a bee brought Sam's attention back to earth as it circled his head. Waving the insect away, he quickly ran to the stately oak and began to search for signs that horses and a stagecoach had actually passed there the night before.

"There's gotta be tracks around here someplace," he muttered, crawling through the grass on his knees. But the tall grass remained unbroken alongside the ancient tree.

"What are ya doing there, laddie?" A voice with a faint Scottish brogue boomed above him. A cane wacked the grass near Sam.

Startled, Sam sprang to his feet. He had been so absorbed with his search that he didn't notice old Mr. Brooks come his way.

"Did I scare ya?" Mr. Brooks smiled, revealing strong white teeth. He leaned on his cane and winked.

"No!" Sam stammered. "I just didn't see you. I was looking for something." He wondered how such a big man could walk right up behind a person and not be heard.

"What are ya searching for?"

"Hoof prints and wheel tracks," Sam mumbled as he dropped to his knees again to continue his search, "from a stagecoach."

The old man stood silent for a moment as he scratched his white beard. "A stagecoach? Why, there hasn't been a coach in these parts since the old inn was running."

"There was an inn here?" Sam asked.

"Nay, not here, over there." He pointed with his cane. "Across the road. Ya can just make out the old foundation."

Sam looked to where Mr. Brooks pointed. "I always thought that was the foundation of a barn. When was it an inn?"

The old man leaned heavily on his cane again. “A long time ago. Let me see. I’d say about ’60. Might have been a little earlier.”

Sam mentally counted. “That was a while ago. My grandpa never told me anything about an inn.”

Mr. Brooks’ laughter filled the air. “Nay, laddie! Not 1960, but 1860! Blue Heron Inn, it was called. Aye, I remember ma’ daddy telling me ghost stories about the ruins. He an’ his brother used to play there as lads, before it came down for good. I used to dig through the rubble when I was younger than you, looking for treasure. The ghost stories were meant to keep me away, but they didn’t. In truth, there was always a bit of a strange story about the place, something about missing people and a murder.”

“Murder?” Sam’s eyes widened. Now that was something! Sam loved mysteries, especially ones that had murder in them. He knew his mother didn’t like him to watch them. They almost always gave him nightmares. But Sam loved them just the same.

“Aye, lots of strange goings on around here then. But I don’t know anything else about it. I was very young when ma’ daddy sent me back to Scotland for ma’ education. The rubble was gone when I returned, and so was ma’ daddy.”

Sam looked up at the old man who appeared to be lost in his memories. Shading his eyes from the sun, Sam then stared across the field to the road where the inn once stood. He tried to imagine what it would have looked like.

“I’m sure there be newspaper clips about the inn at the Mount Marcus library, if ya have a mind to know more,” Mr. Brooks volunteered.

Sam didn’t comment on Mr. Brooks’ suggestion. “Boy, that was a long time ago, huh?” Sam whispered.

“Aye, and that ol’ barn of yours was also part of the inn,” he informed Sam.

“Our barn?” he said incredulously.

The old man nodded.

“Wow!” Sam slowly scanned the immense structure. From a distance, the barn’s cracked and broken upper windows made it look like a toothless giant smiling down on the fields.

"Well, laddie," Mr. Brooks announced as he turned to leave, "I'll be seeing ya." He left quickly, leaving Sam to stare at his grandpa's barn and wonder what it would have looked like in those days.

That afternoon, Sam jumped at the chance to go to Mount Marcus when his mother announced that she had to go shopping. Sam usually avoided going with her to any store, as she would take forever to choose even what kind of cereal to buy. But, as he wanted to go to the library, he climbed into the car with her.

Mount Marcus wasn't a very big town, but it was old. Mohawk Indians first settled the area. The town hall displayed a lot of native artifacts, and a special glass case at the entrance of the library held a few pieces. Normally, Sam would have stopped to study them, but this time he had more important things on his mind.

He approached the desk where the librarian catalogued a large stack of books. "Hello, Miss Timcoe."

"Why, Samuel," the woman said with surprise. "I haven't seen you in quite a while. I thought maybe you had moved away."

"We did," he replied, "up to my grandpa's place in Ivers."

"Oh, that's nice. What can I do for you?"

"I'm looking for a book or newspaper article to tell me about things that happened around here a long time ago." Sam searched his mind for the date. "During the 1850s or so."

"I see," the librarian responded. "That information is kept downstairs in Special Collections. We have quite a few books on the history of the area."

Excited, Sam smiled and turned toward the stairway.

"But," Miss Timcoe reminded him, "you have to have adult supervision to go down there."

Sam's heart sank with disappointment. How could he find out about the inn and the mystery of the magnifying glass if he couldn't get into Special Collections?

Miss Timcoe smiled and continued, "I think Ellie is down there doing some filing. I'll just call down and see if she'll keep an eye on you or help you if you need it."

Sam had made it half way to the stairs before he remembered to thank Miss Timcoe.

Sam found dozens of local history books to look through, and his impatience grew with the flip of each musty page. He finally gave up on the books and decided to ask Ellie if she could help him locate the newspaper archives.

"You should find all kinds of articles on local events in this section," the assistant informed him while showing him where to look.

Sam waited until Ellie returned to her work before he began his search. Finally, after an hour, Sam found it. He took a deep breath to calm his excitement and read:

Mount Marcus Weekly June 10, 1922

BODIES FOUND IN BLUE HERON INN RUINS

Workers in Ivers discovered the skeletal remains of two bodies in the basement of the old Blue Heron Inn ruins yesterday. The workers were in the process of demolishing the inn after the city deemed the property unsafe when a local boy seriously injured himself playing there this past spring.

Built in 1843 by Ezera Titus, the Blue Heron Inn served as a stagecoach stop when he extended his line from Albany to the Canadian border. Upon his death, ownership of the inn passed to his spinster niece, Maggie Hall. Mistress Hall continued the operation of both the stagecoach line and the Blue Heron Inn until the summer of 1860 when the inn burned down. It is believed that Miss Hall chose to leave Ivers for San Francisco, in haste by some recollections, rather than rebuild.

Examiners have determined that the remains are quite old, likely from the time of the fire. Unable to identify either victim, local officials plan to have them interred as anonymous in the Mount Marcus cemetery. Anyone with information is urged to contact Sergeant Connally in Mount Marcus.

Sam read the article again. "Wow, and this happened right near my own house!" His mind whirled with *what ifs* as he sat on the steps of the library and waited for his mother. "What if," he murmured, "one of my ancestors worked or stayed at that inn?"

Though he wondered about the possibility of his ancestors being connected with the inn, Sam waited until they were nearly home before he asked his mother any questions about them. He didn't feel comfortable asking about the past because they were still sad about losing his father, and he didn't want to upset his mother. But he wanted to know, and so he took a deep breath and asked, "Where were you and Dad born?"

Her thoughts must have been elsewhere because she made him repeat the question before she finally answered. "Down in the Hudson Valley. Why?"

"And Grandpa Hobbs? Where was he born?"

"Oh, I don't know … wait. I remember hearing that your father's people came from California someplace."

"California! I wonder why they moved here."

"You'll have to ask your grandfather about that. Why all the sudden interest in the family?"

"I just wanted to know," he said as he turned back toward the window. He wished he had thought to get a copy of the newspaper article to show his grandfather. Sam knew that Grandpa would be able to tell him something about the inn and the skeletons.

Sam had to suspend his investigation while he helped his mother put away the groceries, hang the laundry, and clean his room. It was late afternoon before he could go to the barn. The article about the inn had excited him. With the magnifying glass tucked in his shirt, his digging trowel in hand, and his penlight keychain in his pocket, he returned to the granary in the barn.

Pulling up the board under which he had found the magnifying glass, Sam leaned over the hole and hoped to find something else. As he started to dig, a spray of dirt flew up into his face. He dropped the trowel and rubbed his tearing eye. But rubbing only made it worse. He knew he'd have to see his eye to get the dirt out. Looking around, he spotted a mirror on a nail by the double doors. It was cracked and hung lopsided, but it would still work. Sam stood before it, but he couldn't see anything clearly in the old, yellowish glass. "Ah!" he cried as he remembered his magnifying glass. He pulled it from his shirt and held it up between his face and the mirror.

The magnifying glass made it easy to see the dirt that scratched his eye. Just as he removed the speck with the corner of his shirt-tail, the whole barn suddenly shook with such violence that it knocked him to the floor.

"Oh my gosh," he yelled, "it's an earthquake!" The barn pitched and rolled. Sam managed to crawl to the door frame and sat with his face down against his knees. As abruptly as the quaking had started, it stopped. Any thoughts of his sore eye left him as he slowly stood.

Sam knew immediately that something was wrong. He could feel it; everything seemed different. The very air smelled different. Then he caught sight of the mirror that he had stared into a moment before. No longer cracked and yellow, the glass looked new and sparkling clear. The strangeness didn't stop with the mirror. Everything he saw looked new. The sagging stairs to the upper storage room, the ones he wouldn't climb because they were wobbly, were now firm and straight. Sharp and gleaming tools, harnesses, and straps hung from the beams and walls. Wooden implements that he couldn't identify leaned against crates as if they had just been used.

A strange, queasy feeling churned in the pit of Sam's stomach. He glanced out the window that overlooked his back yard. The tin shed that housed the lawn mower, tools, cans of gasoline, and his ten-speed bike wasn't there. He slowly turned his head toward the house. But the house, his house, Grandpa's house, was gone!

Chapter Two

"Oh my gosh!" Sam called out. "Where's my house?" Where his house had been, he saw only an open field. Then he saw it. Just across the road from his grandfather's property stood a building that he had never seen before. It was a large white house with a second story porch. Above the porch hung a sign that read, "Blue Heron Inn."

Sam slumped to the floor; his mind whirled in confusion. What had happened? Everything that was part of his grandfather's farm had changed, and now an inn had materialized from nowhere. How? He looked at the magnifying glass in his hand. It, too, had transformed into something new. P.W.'s initials seemed deeper and easier to read. He looked closely at the magnifying glass and frowned as he tried to understand. He recalled how, when viewing through the glass the night before, he had seen the strange stagecoach. He had even seen a man inside. Then he thought of the last thing he did before the barn shook. He had looked through the glass into the mirror to remove the dirt in his eye.

"The magnifying glass!" he cried. He knew that somehow it held the answer to the strange events.

"If I look back through this, maybe everything will be the same as it was," he reasoned.

He moved back to the mirror and started to raise the glass to his face again. But then he stopped. Curiosity took hold of him. This could be an adventure, and Sam loved adventures even more than he loved mysteries. He began to wonder what this place was like. Who lived here? Would he meet the original owners of the farm? And what about the disappearances and murder that Mr. Brooks mentioned? He lowered the glass. He could return any time he wanted, as long as he had the glass. Why not just take a little look around? What harm could it do?

Sam shoved the magnifying glass back into his waist. He then gathered his courage and exited the barn. He glanced down both sides of the field. Not seeing anyone, he headed for the inn. Half way there, a stagecoach rushed by him. His heart thumped with excitement as he chased after it. The driver stopped the coach in front of the inn's entrance. Not wanting to be seen, Sam darted behind a vine-covered trellis at the side of the building. He wedged himself between the vines and the house; his breath almost stopped from the thrill. He wondered what to do next. Stay hidden? Show himself?

He still couldn't believe that he stood next to a building that didn't really exist. He reached out and touched the side of it, almost afraid that it might disappear on contact. But it didn't. He glanced up at the cracked and weathered sign. The painted outlines of two birds, blue herons he assumed, had become almost indistinguishable underneath the fading letters.

He heard voices, and so he found a peep-hole in the vines and watched as the passengers disembarked from the coach. A small woman, wrapped in a black cloak and wearing long gloves, exited first. A black veil completely covered her head and shoulders. Sam felt sorry for her. He couldn't imagine anyone wearing so many clothes in the summer. He assumed that she was an old widow because of the black garments and the way she stooped over. A short, spindly-legged man in a yellow and black checkered suit exited next. Though a brown derby hat shadowed most of his face, Sam could still see that the man had a thin mustache and a deep frown that pulled his bushy eyebrows together. The third passenger, a man with a black top hat and matching black suit, stuck his head out the door. Before disembarking, he snapped his head around and looked directly at the trellis, as if he could see Sam through the vines.

"Oh my gosh," Sam declared, flattening himself against the wall, "it's him!" His stomach flipped and his throat tightened. The third passenger was the very same man that he had seen in the magnifying glass the night before. Now the man stood not more than twenty feet away from him. Sam's legs trembled. A sudden and unexplainable fear washed over him.

When he got the courage to look again, he saw that the man stood away from the coach with his back to him. The man in the yellow suit pointed into the carriage and said something to the woman. Instead of answering him, she handed him a card. Having barely glanced at it, the man tossed it to the ground. A breeze caught the underside of the card, and it fluttered and skidded under the vines. It landed face up within inches of Sam's feet. It read, "I AM MUTE." He pulled his feet back as far as he could when he saw the woman come toward him to retrieve the card. As she reached under the vines, the veil parted from her face and showed that she wasn't old at all. She was a young black girl. Sam figured that she couldn't have been more than fourteen years old. He wondered why the mute girl dressed like an old widow. He couldn't imagine anyone that young being married or widowed.

A loud cheery voice drew Sam's attention. "Welcome to the Blue Heron Inn, folks. I'm Maggie Hall."

Sam stuck his head around the trellis to see a rather plump woman come down the front steps. He liked the look of her immediately. She reminded him of his beloved great aunt, which he always termed with a smile as "soft and squishy." Then he stopped as he tried to recall where he had seen that name before. Had he heard correctly? Maggie Hall. He remembered the newspaper article that he had read in the library. Maggie Hall was the name of Ezera Titus' niece. Sam had been so taken by all that he saw and experienced that he hadn't given much thought as to *when* he experienced it. The newspaper article mentioned that Maggie Hall had left the inn during the summer of 1860. "Wow," he uttered softly, "this must be just before the Civil War."

He would have pondered this information further, but Maggie called to the driver, "Bud, I'm a little short-handed today. Will you bring the luggage in for me?"

"I'm on a tight schedule, Maggie," the driver complained, "I gotta get going right-a-way."

"I've just taken a pie from the oven," she coaxed.

The driver scratched his beard and replied, "I guess I could spare a minute." He climbed down off the coach. "You there, Mr. Malis," he called to the black-suited man, "would ya mind lending me a hand? You can take the lady's bag."

Malis! So that's his name, Sam thought. It sure fit him. He certainly looked full of malice.

Malis moved back to the coach, his thin face pinched with apparent irritation as he pulled the smallest bag off the top rack and carried it onto the porch.

"You folks come on in," Maggie said, holding the door open. "I'll show you to your rooms. Supper is at seven sharp, and I appreciate promptness."

As she turned fully into Sam's view, he studied her round, friendly face. Her eyes twinkled with the same sort of kindness that he saw in his great aunt's eyes. She had to be the kind of person that a lost boy shouldn't be afraid of. But as he looked at the thin, dark Mr. Malis, Sam became leery of approaching her or entering the inn. He decided he would wait to try to speak with Maggie Hall later after the guests went to their rooms. He sat on the ground, his stomach rumbling from hunger. It had been a long time since lunch. "What am I going to do?" he muttered.

"I'll tell you what you're gonna do," a deep voice suddenly commanded above and behind him. Before Sam could move, thick hands grabbed his shoulders and pulled him to his feet.

"OW! What are you doing?" Sam yelled. "Let me go!"

As the big man turned him around to face him, Sam's shirt came untucked and his prized treasure fell to the ground. Frowning, the man picked up the magnifying glass, tightening his hold on Sam as he did so.

"You little thief!" he shouted as he started to shake Sam.

"I'm no thief!" Sam protested as he tried to get free of the man's hold.

"Then what are you doing with Mr. Wilson's missing magic glass?"

"Magic glass? I don't know what you're talking about! I found this in the … in the …" But how could he explain to the angry man not so much *where* he had actually found the glass, but *when*?

"Well, I'd say we've got us a thief all right." He pulled Sam around the trellis and onto the porch. He then shoved him through the front door of the inn where the veiled girl and driver stood while they waited for Maggie to finish registering the guests.

Maggie looked up from behind the desk near the door. "Otis," she said curtly, "what are you doing to that child?"

"This young'un stole Mr. Wilson's magic glass," Otis declared, holding both Sam and the magic glass out in front of him.

"I did not!" Sam shouted. "I'm no thief!" He wiggled free and stood angrily before them, ready to run if the man tried to grab him again.

Maggie frowned as she rounded the desk and stood before Sam. "Then where did you get it, boy?"

Sam looked at the faces surrounding him. The stagecoach driver impatiently blew his nose in his handkerchief, the veiled girl clutched her purse tightly in her hands while she shifted nervously from one foot to the other, and Otis' glare never wavered. Sam suddenly felt like he had been given detention for cheating but couldn't prove his innocence. None of them would believe him. At least the man named Malis wasn't there, as Sam figured the creepy man would probably call for a hanging.

"I … I found it," Sam finally stuttered. "I told the man that, but he wouldn't listen to me."

"Where?" Maggie inquired, her voice becoming softer.

"Out in the barn," his words trailed off to a whisper, "a little while ago."

"Hmmm," Maggie murmured. Sam could clearly see that she didn't believe him. She reached out and took Sam gently by his shoulders. He didn't pull away. "Paul Wilson got that glass from an old medicine man who said that it did powerful things. Mr. Wilson uses it in his magic show that he puts on in the barn every year. I don't think he'd be misplacing something as special as that, do you?" Not giving Sam a chance to answer, she turned to Otis, "You take Mr. Wilson's glass up to Mr. Malis, as he's Mr. Wilson's new assistant. Mr. Wilson won't be back until after supper."

"NO!" Sam yelled as he lunged for the magnifying glass.

But Maggie grabbed his arm. "Boy," she said sharply, "you're old enough to understand that you can't have what's not yours. Now come along with me." She turned to the driver, "I won't be a minute, Bud, so please take Mrs. Moses up to her room and then come on down to the kitchen for pie."

"Thanks, Maggie, but I really gotta git now," Bud replied. "I'll take these things up and see your guest to her room. I'll see you on the next run."

Maggie nodded in agreement and started to pull Sam along with her.

Panic over losing the magnifying glass grabbed hold of Sam, but try as he may, he couldn't get free of Maggie. "You don't understand," Sam whined, "I can't get back without that glass."

"I understand one thing," Maggie said crossly, "you have a lot of explaining to do." With Sam in tow, she stormed through the dining room and into the kitchen.

Maggie's kitchen was twice the size of his grandfather's kitchen. Oddly, there weren't any appliances, refrigerator, electric stove, dishwasher, or even counters. Two very large tables with chairs, two cabinets at least six feet tall, and a massive black iron stove dominated the large room. Big pots, with lids that softly clinked up and down as puffs of steam emitted from them, covered the stove surface. An iron shelf lined with pint-sized salt and pepper shakers and a stack of pot holders jetted out over the back row of pots. A small tin box full of wooden matches hung on the wall next to the stove. Several loaves of freshly baked bread filled a rack near the back door. On one of the tables sat four pies and a tray of what looked like turnovers. The assortment of smells made Sam's mouth water, and he rubbed his stomach.

Maggie glanced at him. As if knowing that a hungry boy is more likely to get into mischief, she cut a piece of fresh cherry pie, placed it on a plate, and pushed it in front of him. "Sit yourself down and eat this," she said. Then she sat down across from him. "Now, boy, tell me your name, where you come from, why you're dressed so funny, and what you were doing in my barn."

Sam took several mouthfuls of pie before answering. She might take the pie away if she didn't like his answers. But Maggie waited patiently.

"My name is Sam, and I live … I'm from the circus," he said. "Yes, a travelling circus." He felt clever; it was definitely a good answer to explain his modern clothes and sneakers. "And I was in your barn because … because …" What was he going to say? He couldn't admit the real reason or she'd think he was crazy. Sam began to panic because he remembered reading about how doctors treated crazy people before they considered insanity an actual illness. He wanted no part of being put in an asylum. "Because I saw a puppy go in there. A real cute puppy," he hurriedly added. It was a huge lie, but he hoped Maggie would believe it.

Maggie listened as she wiped crumbs off the tablecloth. Then she said, "Boy, I think you're hiding something. You look too well cared-for to be a runaway from the circus. I'll let you go home if you tell me the truth about that magnifying glass."

"But I can't go home!" Sam exclaimed truthfully.

"Then I'll send Otis for your parents to come and fetch you. I'm sure they'll be wondering where you've gotten to."

"No, you can't. My … my family was killed in an accident. A fire. A big fire down near the city. I've been looking out for myself since." Sam had to stop her questions until he could come up with a good explanation about the glass, and this seemed like the best way. He thought this horrid lie might just work. He wasn't used to lying. His mother always knew when he did, and she would punish him more for the lie than for what he lied about. So he learned early not to do it.

Maggie looked at him, and her face softened. "I'm so sorry, Sam."

As Sam looked into Maggie's dark eyes, he felt the blood drain from his face. That lie was way too horrible. How was he going to get out of this if she pressed for more details? Lie again? He hung his head and knew he'd never be able to pull off such deceitfulness.

Fortunately, Maggie stopped her questions and said, "Well, I won't take the place of your poor mother, but I could certainly use some help. My hired boy didn't show this morning, and, as you seem to need a place to stay, you can stay here for a few days. Besides, I feel there's more to you, orphaned circus boy, than meets the eye."

For a moment, Sam just looked at her. He didn't want to risk losing track of Paul Wilson's magnifying glass. He arrived there with it, and he needed it to return home. There was nothing else he could do. He had to stay. "All right," he replied.

"Then it's settled," Maggie said, getting up from the table. "Now where can I put you? I do have an open bed in the third room on the right up the back stairs." She pointed to the stairs across the kitchen between the pantry door and the archway to the dining room. "That will have to be yours. Mr. Wilson has the room across from you, and Mr. Malis is further up the hall. Our lady visitor has the very front room. I won't tolerate you disturbing my guests, so be quiet any time you're up there. You understand?"

Sam nodded. He had no intentions of disturbing the guests, especially not Malis.

Going into the pantry, Maggie returned carrying a pitcher covered with a cloth. "Here, this should chase down that pie real good," she said, filling a mug.

As Maggie placed the remainder of the pie back on the table and covered it with a cloth, Sam took a mouthful of the liquid. It came out as fast as it went in. Spitting it out, Sam cried, "Oh my gosh, what is this stuff? It tastes awful!"

"Awful?" Maggie took the mug from him and sniffed it. "It shouldn't taste bad," she said. "It's fresh, straight from the cow this morning."

"The COW!" Sam yelled, his face scrunched in disgust.

"Yes! Only I did skim the fat off to make a fresh ball of butter, so maybe that's why it tastes funny to you. Sometimes milk does taste funny without the fat."

"I'll … I'll have a glass of water instead please," Sam said as he looked around for the water faucets.

"You're quite fussy for a boy with no folks, aren't you? But if you have a taste for water, it's on the porch. You'll find the barrel to the right and the ladle on the peg above it."

Sam didn't move, but his mouth dropped open. He never drank water out of a barrel before, and he wasn't sure he wanted to do so now.

Maggie seemed to notice his hesitation. "I'll get it for you this time, Sam, but you'll have to get things for yourself from now on. Shyness isn't a good sign of character, especially in a boy." She left and soon returned with a cup of water. "I won't tolerate laziness, either. Everyone works for their keep, and you'll be no different. Have you ever milked a cow?"

"No." Sam liked to think he had spunk enough to take on almost any challenge, but the idea of milking a cow seemed disgusting.

She took Sam's hands into hers and turned their palms up. "Judging by your hands, I'd say you've never done a lick of hard work in your life. These are the cleanest and smoothest hands I've ever seen on a boy." Maggie shook her head, muttering something about children today being ill equipped for the world. Then she continued, "I'll take you up to the barn and let Otis decide what chores you're to do. He'll watch over you while I've gone to Mr. Thatcher's. I don't want you idly sitting by when you can help out, so do as Otis tells you."

Sam didn't like the idea of being left with Otis. Aside from Otis being mean, the man thought he was a thief. "Do I have to work with him?" Sam whined, "Isn't there something I can do here in the inn?"

"No!" And that was all she said. Taking a firm hold of Sam's arm, Maggie led him to the barn.

Chapter Three

Both Otis and the job of shoveling manure were unpleasant. The big man never stopped watching him the entire time. Sam had never worked so hard in his life. After a couple of hours of mucking and hauling, he wanted nothing more than to just sit down. A few times he even tried to sneak away, but Otis' glaring stare and the threat to "wrap him with balling wire and hang him from the rafters for the rest of the day" took all the courage out of Sam. Besides mumbling under his breath, the only talking Otis did was to order Sam around, telling him what shovel to use for the manure, what cart to put it in, and where to get the fresh hay for the horse stalls after they'd been cleaned.

Just when Sam thought he had done everything that needed to be done, Otis gave him one last job. He handed Sam a wide broom and bellowed, "You gotta stack those bags of feed along the walls and sweep out the center of that room in there." Pointing to the granary, he said, "I want ya to line them bales of hay up into rows so people can sit and watch Wilson's magic show tonight."

All the tension and tiredness dissipated from Sam, and he excitedly asked, "A magic show?"

"Yup, and it ain't a show to be missed, so git at it!"

Sam dragged the heavy sacks of grain to the wall and swept the center of the granary floor. He only paused briefly to catch his breath. He couldn't wait to see the show. Wilson would have the magnifying glass with him. Somehow, Sam had to get it back in order to go home. The adventure had worn off, and Sam felt both physically and mentally tired. He was indeed ready to leave.

Otis sat no more than a couple yards away, rubbing oil into a harness, and he still didn't take his eyes off Sam. Sam had tried to be nice to the gruff man. He smiled, said "yes, sir," and worked as hard as he could. But nothing Sam did lessened Otis' hostility toward him. Finally, Sam quit trying. More than likely, he concluded, Otis would treat him the same way even if he didn't think he was a thief. He knew that some adults were just like that. Sam mumbled, "He probably doesn't even remember being a kid."

Frowning, Otis grumbled, "What ya say, boy?"

"Nothing."

"Umph, well, get on back to see if Maggie has any more work for you to do." As Sam pushed the last bale of hay into place, Otis hung the harness on a hook and left the barn without a word.

Glad to be finished, Sam ran to the inn. But Maggie wasn't there, nor anyone else. Sam went back out on the porch and sat to wait for someone to show up. Sitting with only the crickets' songs to break the stillness, Sam began to feel uneasy. More than once he caught himself looking over his shoulder and thinking someone stood there. Maybe he found the silence a little too eerie, or maybe he just felt out of place in a time not his own. If he were home now, his mother would be telling him to wash up for supper. She'd ask him to set the table or fill their glasses with ice tea. Then she'd serve him dinner and they'd talk about their day. He realized how hungry he had become. But he wouldn't let himself think about home or his hunger because he couldn't do anything about either one. A short while later, Sam grew relieved to see Maggie approach, carrying a basket.

"Here, Sam," she said as she handed him the basket, "take these around to the pump and rinse them off. I swapped two loaves of my nutmeat bread and a quart of apple relish for them. Did you ever see such big berries? When I saw them, I got a hankering for my favorite pie. Do you like strawberry rhubarb pie?"

"Yes, I sure do!" he said cheerfully.

She smiled. "Come on, then. Get a move on or we won't be having any after dinner."

While Maggie started supper and made the pies, Sam peeled, chopped, and brought in water and wood for the stove. This kind of work suited him better. He'd much rather be in the kitchen than in the barn working with manure. As Sam finished his last wood trip, he began to grow more excited about the show. He wondered if Wilson would perform some kind of magic he hadn't seen already. He liked to watch magic shows and specials, but this show had to be at least fifteen years before the great Houdini's birth, and long before special effects.

Maggie sliced the ham and dished some potatoes and vegetables into serving bowls. Then she put a generous portion on a plate and placed it on a tray.

"Sam," she addressed him, "the guest in the front-most room upstairs won't be coming down for supper. Take the tray up to her room and put it on the floor in front of the door. Knock twice, then leave immediately. Don't dally. Do you understand?"

"Yes, ma'am," he answered as he took the tray from her.

Sam had forgotten about the mute girl he had seen earlier. As he climbed the stairs and took his time walking the long hallway, he wondered about her. It seemed strange that she had kept hidden behind a veil and then disappeared into her room as soon as she arrived at the inn. He wondered why such a young girl would be wearing a veil at all. She looked pretty enough, and she wasn't disfigured. He wondered why she didn't want to be seen. Then Sam felt stupid as he suddenly realized the reason: by 1860, slavery had become the main issue of the day. He had learned in class that the eleven Southern states that formed the Confederate States of America fought to keep slavery alive. Balancing the tray, he moved slowly down the hall. Sam concluded that she had good reason to wear a disguise, because she probably was a runaway slave. But, he wondered, what was she doing here? Where was she going? Sam then recalled that the Canadian border lay only fifteen miles north. A quiver of excitement ran through him. He wasn't about to just set the tray on the floor and leave as Maggie told him to do. He couldn't miss this chance to meet her.

His knocks on the door echoed through the hall so loudly that Sam thought Maggie might hear it down in the kitchen. He moved to the side of the doorway, out of view. After a moment, he heard the key turn in the lock and the door crack open.

"Don't be afraid," he said as soon as he saw her, "I brought your supper."

The girl, still heavily veiled and wearing gloves, pointed to the table by the bed.

As he set the tray down, Sam couldn't control his excitement any longer and blurted out, "You're not an old widow woman, are you?"

With a horrified gasp, the girl suddenly grabbed his arm with an unexpectedly strong grasp and tried to force him from the room. To Sam's surprise, she almost succeeded in pushing him through the doorway.

"Wait a minute," he pleaded, "I only want to talk."

The girl slowly released him, but she didn't speak or move.

Sam looked in the hallway and then closed the door. He strained to see her face though the thick veil. "You're a runaway slave, aren't you?"

She didn't answer. Instead, she snatched the knife off the tray and lunged at him.

"Hey!" he yelled. He dodged the knife and tried to grab her wrist. "Are you crazy? I don't want to turn you over to the law! Put that thing down!"

She lunged again and slashed through the air like a wild woman. Sam grew terrified. The blade barely missed him. Before she could get her balance to swing again, Sam landed a lucky blow to her wrist and knocked the knife from her hand. As she scrambled to retrieve it, she tripped and went sprawling across the floor. Sam threw himself on her back and pinned her arms to the floor.

"I swear," he panted, trying to keep her from escaping his hold, "I'm not going to turn you over to anybody." He wanted to gain her trust. "And you have to promise not to tell anybody about me. I've run away from my home and don't belong here, either. I'm almost a captive now." But the girl still fought to get free, so he admitted to her, "If I was going to turn you in, I could have done it earlier when you first got off the stagecoach. I saw your face when you picked up the mute card that guy threw on the ground." His words must have hit home because the girl stopped struggling. The muscles in her arms relaxed. Sam breathed easier. "I should have known that pretending to be mute was part of a disguise," he said, trying to calm the shakiness in his voice. "That was pretty smart. That way no one could detect your age or pretty much anything about you." He loosened his grip on her a little. She didn't move. "I'll let you up if you promise not to try and kill me again."

She nodded, and Sam let go. They sat on the floor and just looked at each other.

"Ya ain't no slave," she finally said as she slipped her veil off and exposed her face.

She was young, Sam observed, probably not much older than himself. She had large brown eyes and thick dark braids wound tightly up in a bun.

"Why would anyone be after you?" she asked. "Wha'd ya do, kill somebody?"

"No, of course not!"

"Ya said ya was being held captive here."

"Yeah, kind of. I'm stuck here because they took something from me, and I can't go home until I get it back." He extended his hand for her to shake. "My name's Sam, and I'm twelve."

"I'm Cassy," she said, frowning at his outstretched hand. "An' I think I'm older 'an that, but I ain't sure. Nobody ever told me when I was born."

Sam lowered his hand and smiled. "I'll tell you about myself if you'll tell me about yourself."

Cassy eyed Sam for a minute, and then she said, "Ya can go first." She sat at the table and picked up her fork.

Sam put the knife on the table and sat on the bed. As he watched Cassy eat, he wanted to tell her about the Civil War, the Emancipation Proclamation, and all the future, but then he thought better of it. Instead, he told her the truth about the magnifying glass and how he suddenly found himself there. Hearing himself speak, Sam realized that the truth was funnier than any story.

Try as she could, Cassy couldn't take Sam seriously, and she started to laugh. She laughed until tears rolled down her face. "Boy, you's a tall taler, ain't ya? But that's all good 'cause anybody that's got that kind a funnin' in him ain't mean enough to turn me over to the law."

Sam laughed as well, then asked, "What about you? Where are you from?"

Swallowing her last bite, Cassy wiped her mouth on her sleeve and shoved the empty plate away from her. Born in South Carolina, she had been abused by her master and by anyone who had any authority over her. She escaped with a group nearly two months prior. Most didn't make it out of the woods, but some made it to a safe house. They spent the next few weeks moving mostly at night from house to house. On the night they were supposed to cross the Potomac River, men surrounded their house and burned everyone out. The lady of the house grabbed Cassy and managed to get her across the river. Cassy's older sister had also been in that house that night, and Cassy didn't know if she were alive or dead.

Sam suddenly felt as if all of his problems were silly. "It must have been very scary to run away."

She sighed. "They whipped me if I did my work, an' they whipped me if I didn't," she said matter-of-factly. She bared her arms. Ugly red scars marked both her wrists. Then she bent her head down and traced her finger along a white scar on her neck. Cassy told him that she got that when the overseer's wife had hit her with a hot poker for not cooking the food well enough. "Ya get used to that life, but ya never accept it. There's more to livin' than whippin's. I want to get learnin'. I want to be able to work, an' spend my own money, an' go where I want without sneakin'. I want to own my own land. I want to be free. As long as I'm a slave, I ain't never gonna get to do none of them things."

Her words saddened and appalled him to the point of speechlessness. It was one thing to read about slaves in books, but it was another thing to meet someone who had been a slave and to see her scars. "I'm so sorry, Cassy," he finally said.

"What ya done to be sorry about? It ain't like ya did the whippin'."

But that's exactly how Sam felt, guilty and sorry for her and anyone in that situation. He would have liked to have talked with Cassy more, but he suddenly heard Maggie impatiently calling for him. He rose. "Are you going to the magic show later?" he asked as he moved toward the door.

Shaking her head, Cassy answered, "No, it's too dangerous for me."

"Oh, of course," he replied. "I better go. I hope you get to Canada soon, Cassy."

"Me, too. I hope ya gets back to your home," she giggled, "where 'er 'tis."

Sam left the room, and he stayed in the hall until he heard the key turn in the lock.

Dinner lasted an eternity. The adults talked a great deal about the coming presidential election. Though anxious for the magic show,

Sam became engrossed in what everyone had to say about the likely candidates, especially Abraham Lincoln. If only he could record the conversation. What a grade he would get in history class! But then, who'd believe him?

"What do you think, Ephil?" Otis asked. "What will happen if Lincoln wins?"

Sam almost dropped his fork when Malis answered. *Ephil* so closely resembled *evil* that Sam decided it fit the man accurately.

Maggie cornered Sam after supper and put him to work washing the dishes. He wasted no time running to the barn as soon as she let him go.

As he approached, he saw Otis in the granary with Ephil Malis and another man. The unknown man had to be Paul Wilson. Malis turned from the others and looked toward the barn doors. Instinctively, Sam ducked away. Since it appeared that Malis stood guard, Sam decided to stay out until other people arrived. He dragged a wooden crate to the window, climbed upon it, and watched as the men set up a make-shift stage. Sam's heart all but stood still as Wilson took the magnifying glass out from his oversized pocket and placed it on a table in the middle of the stage.

"There it is!" Sam uttered. He pressed his hand against the window. "I have to find a way to get it back."

He had no sooner said those words when a prickly feeling slowly crept across his neck. He didn't have to turn around to know that Ephil Malis stood behind him. But Sam did turn. As he did, his foot crashed through the slates of the crate, and his ankle became painfully wedged between the jagged and broken boards. Malis started toward him. The closer he came to Sam, the faster Sam's heart raced. He tried to reason that the man only wanted to help him, but he knew that wasn't true. He had a feeling that if Malis ever got his hands on him, it would be all over for him; he wouldn't get the glass, and he'd never get home.

Then, as if in answer to a prayer, a bunch of excited kids suddenly appeared and clustered around Malis. Malis stopped and greeted the children, but he continued to glare at Sam. Before Malis turned away, his lips seemed to form the words, "Another time, boy."

Sam shivered in fear and then finally pried his foot loose from the crate. Like a pied piper with a painted smile, Ephil Malis led the kids into the barn, performing small feats of magic as he walked.

Nervous flutters attacked Sam's stomach as he joined the crowd gathered in front of the barn doors. It had taken all his courage to stay and attend the magic show after his encounter with Malis. Sam continued to watch Ephil Malis closely. He watched as Malis charmed them all: the kids, the mothers, and the fathers. Maggie also seemed charmed by him. That worried Sam the most. Having seen the evil in Malis' eyes, Sam vowed not to be taken in by him. He waited to enter the barn until just before the show began.

As it grew dark, the flickering of the lamp light cast eerie shadows over the interior of the barn. The audience became spellbound by the performance. Sam almost forgot about his dilemma as he watched the show, until Malis rolled a black box, like a coffin standing on end, out onto the center of the stage. Sam had seen those boxes before, hundreds of times. They were disappearing boxes; all the magicians used them.

Malis walked to the front of the stage and said, "I need a volunteer to help with our next trick. Do I have any takers?" Ignoring all the excited children who raised their hands, he pointed to Sam. "You there, the boy in the strangely colored shirt, how about you?"

Sam knew Malis meant him, for he had the only yellow, orange, and red plaid shirt in the room. Everybody else wore blue, brown, or grey colored clothing. But he was not going to submit himself to Ephil Malis or his magic box. Ignoring the cries of encouragement from the crowd, Sam leaned back as far as he could on the hay bale and shook his head. Malis leered down at him, then reluctantly chose another child. With a sigh of relief, Sam watched a little girl go up on stage. The trick, of course, succeeded. Sam knew it wouldn't have if he had been the one to get into that box.

Wilson performed the next act. He donned a long black robe, picked up the magnifying glass, and held it up for all to see. The lamps seemed to dim as he started to speak.

"This magnifying glass was given to me by the spirit of Hiawatha, the great Onondaga leader, dead now for over two hundred years. It was given to him by the Spirit of the Moon." At this point, Wilson paused while a stage hand lowered a prop, colored and shaped like a full moon, behind Wilson. Even though Sam knew it was just a hunk of wood painted yellow, the effect mystified him. Wilson continued. "The sacred wooden frame that houses this glass," at this point he traced his hands around the frame, "was carved with the knife that killed Hiawatha's adversary, the mythical white bison. The glass," here he paused to run his fingers over the glass, "was made from the bison's ground-up eyes and stained with its blood." The little girls in the audience gasped in horror, and the boys snickered. "Thus, the glass has received its powers. I once saved the Onondagas from a great calamity, and, in gratitude, they gave this priceless object to me. With it, I can peer into men's souls and see their deepest, darkest secrets."

Sam might have found the magician's spiel corny if he didn't know what that glass could do.

As Wilson continued to speak, the stage lamps dimmed low until they were almost extinguished. To the startled cry of many, a great puff of smoke suddenly filled the stage. When the smoke cleared, there stood, bathed in cool blue light, a robed Onondaga chief, feathers and all. Wilson swayed back and forth as if in a trance.

"Oh, spirit of Hiawatha, speak to me," Wilson chanted.

With a quivering, hollow voice the chief spoke. "The Father of Spirits says a generous man is rewarded in the great resting place of heroes." The chief then pointed to the magnifying glass and turned to the audience. "The glass of wisdom seeks truth."

Another puff of smoke engulfed the ghost, and he disappeared behind the smoke. Wilson then stepped off stage and started moving through the crowd.

"Who among you dares to expose your most inner thoughts to the magic powers of the glass? Do you have the purity or braveness of heart to let me look into your eyes?"

As he went in and out of the aisles, he stood in front of one and then another, but everyone closed their eyes and turned away. Then the magician stopped in front of Sam. "How about it, son, are you brave enough for my magic?"

The crowd applauded. They were more than willing to let Sam be the first. Before Sam could reply, Wilson raised the magnifying glass between his face and Sam's. A murmur spread though the audience as they waited for the magician to reveal what he saw.

As the magician stared through the magnifying glass, a puzzled look came over his features. "What? How come I don't see you?" he whispered to Sam. He put his hand on Sam's shoulder as if to make sure he was there. Again, he raised the glass to look at Sam. "I'll be!" With a confused expression, Wilson lowered the glass and turned to the audience. He stammered slightly. "I saw ... I saw a thief of the neighbor's apples, and, if anyone is missing a pie, here's your culprit."

The spectators laughed as Wilson returned to the stage and gave Sam a long, quizzical look. Sam didn't wait to see the rest of the show. He scrambled quickly out of the barn.

At first it upset Sam that Wilson couldn't see him in the magnifying glass. But the more he thought about it, the plainer it became. Sam wasn't part of that time. To Sam, it proved that the glass did contain the magic that brought him there. If Sam had any doubt before that he needed the magnifying glass to get home, he had none now.

Chapter Four

A rude shake woke Sam before dawn. "We got work to do, thief," Otis stated gruffly. "Git yourself out to the barn."

"What about breakfast?" Sam moaned. "Don't we get to eat first?"

"You eat after the animals do."

Otis left, and Sam fumbled around in the dark for his clothes. He wasn't pleased that the cows were more important than him, but he complied.

After he had cared for the cows and horses and fed the chickens, Sam finally got to eat. Still early, only he, Otis, and Maggie were in the kitchen. She served a huge breakfast of boiled potatoes, steak, and eggs. With the center of a stove lid removed, she then toasted thick slices of homemade bread on a rack. To Sam's delight, she topped off the meal with a piece of apple pie. His mother would never allow him to eat pie for breakfast. He wanted to go back to bed after breakfast, but Maggie had stripped his bed of its sheets. He spent the rest of the morning running water to and from the stove for her to do his sheets and the rest of the laundry. They washed the laundry outside in huge tubs. Maggie scrubbed the clothes on a board that had raised ridges. Then she stirred them with a stick in boiling water. Sam wondered what she'd do if she ever saw his mother's washer and dryer.

Otis wanted the stalls cleaned earlier than usual, so Maggie sent Sam to the barn when she no longer needed him. Sam felt exhausted, but he obeyed as he didn't want to let Maggie down.

The smell of the barn and Otis' temper were both as sour as the day before. Sam cleared the hay bales from the center of the granary floor and put them back where they belonged. As he put the last bale in place, Sam looked around and couldn't see Otis. Normally, being alone would relax Sam, but Sam once again had the feeling of being watched. Yet, whenever he looked around, he saw no one. At one point he had the impression that he heard voices coming from the very wood of the barn itself. Looking over his shoulder for the fourth time, he wondered if it had anything to do with the magic show the previous night. The creepy feeling got the best of him, and he moved to the other end of the barn to clean the stalls there. It took him the rest of the morning to get the unpleasant job done.

Sam rested on the back porch and tried to scrape the manure from his sneakers. It proved difficult to get out, even with a stick. He ended up removing his sneakers. He knew Maggie would not like it if he tracked that stuff in on her floors. For a moment, the thought of Maggie lingered in his mind. Without her there, he would have felt like a lamb in a den of wolves. Then the eerie feeling washed over him again. Grabbing his sneakers, he ran into the kitchen and up the back stairs. The only place he felt free of unseen spying eyes was the safety of his bedroom.

As he walked down the hallway, he heard a swell of angry voices from Wilson's room. Sam stopped a few feet from Wilson's partially opened door, not exactly sure of what to do. If he continued to his room, they'd see him and think that he'd been eavesdropping. If he turned around and went back downstairs, he would likely run into Otis. As the argument between the two men became more heated, Sam did neither. He inched along the shadowy side of the wall, edging closer to their door until he could overhear some of what they said. Whatever they were quarreling about, it sure wasn't magic.

"You can't …" Wilson's voice shouted angrily. "The line …"

Ephil Malis replied, but Sam could only make out a few of his words. "Federal marshal … you coward! Freight … worth thousands!"

Wilson's squeaky voice turned into a screechy howl. "Fool! The station … closed … They KNOW! I won't hang for …"

The exchange devolved into a confusion of sounds, scuffling, and groans. Sam heard a heavy thud, then complete silence.

"Oh my gosh," he gasped as he flattened himself tight against the side of the hall. He had no doubt that something awful had happened. Clinging to the dark wall, he started to ease back toward the stairs, staying in the shadows. He hadn't gone very far when a loose floorboard groaned beneath his feet. At the sound, Wilson's door swung fully open and Malis stepped from the room. His narrow eyes seemed to pierce the very darkness in which Sam stood. Sam panicked and charged down the back stairs. As he jumped the last four steps, he feverishly thought of a place to hide.

"THE PANTRY!" his mind screamed. Heavy footsteps echoed through the staircase. With cunning and speed, Sam rushed across the kitchen to the back door, kicked it open, then raced back across the kitchen to the pantry. He accidentally dropped his sneakers on the kitchen floor as he dove into the large storeroom. Within seconds, he heard Malis' footsteps cross the kitchen. Sam squeezed under the storeroom's bottom shelf along the left wall. He pulled his long legs out of sight and waited for Malis to leave. The door slammed only once. Had Malis gone outside to search for him?

With his shoulders aching from his cramped position, Sam waited for the second slam of the door, but the sound didn't come. His right arm soon went to sleep, leaving his hand numb. But he didn't dare move, even his fingers. He laid there and listened as he strained to identify the tiniest sound. His head began to throb. If only Maggie would come back.

After what seemed like an hour, Sam heard banging and bumping, as if someone had fallen down the stairs. The pantry door suddenly swung open. Sam stifled the scream that threatened to expose him. By the daylight from the kitchen, he saw the thin form of Ephil Malis drag Paul Wilson's plump body into the pantry. Wilson's head bobbed limply from side to side. Sam thought he was going to be sick as the body passed within inches of him. He tried to look away. If Malis found him, he'd soon be as dead as poor Wilson.

Sam saw Malis slide his hand along a narrow firing strip half way up the wall. A portion of the lower wall sprang open and exposed a hidden passage. Malis backed into the darkness and pulled Wilson's body in after him. A series of dull thumps echoed from the passage, and Sam knew by the sound that Malis dragged the body down a flight of stairs. The sound faded until Sam heard nothing more from the dark passageway.

Sam wondered if he should allow his curiosity and sense of adventure to overcome his fear and follow Malis down into the passageway, or if he should stay hidden until Maggie came home. He wondered if the passageway had another exit. As much as the death of Wilson had shaken him, he wasn't about to allow Malis to get away with murder. He scurried out from his hiding place, went through the hidden door, and climbed down the wooden steps. As he moved into the dimness, he recalled that the old newspaper article mentioned two skeletons found in the ruins of the inn. Was Paul Wilson one of them? Sam had to find out, and he prayed that the other skeleton wasn't him.

Cautiously, he made his way down to the bottom of the steps and followed a narrow tunnel. A light shone from a room off to the right, a short distance ahead. The lamp's glow suddenly grew wider and spilled back out into the passage. Sam retreated and ducked under the steps. Malis came out of the room. He held the lantern high over his head as he checked the passageway, but he didn't go back toward the stairs. Instead, he turned and went deeper into the underground passage where both he and the light disappeared.

Sam returned back up the stairs, grabbed the candle holder from the table, and lit the candle from the embers in the stove. He returned to the secret passage. Descending the stairs as quietly as he could, Sam moved stealthily into the musty-smelling room that Malis had vacated.

The room looked to be half the size of the kitchen above. In one corner he saw two cots, a chair, and a rickety table. Why would anyone want to stay down there, in that damp, musty hole? He wondered if Ezera Titus had it dug when he built the inn, and he also wondered if Maggie even knew about it.

He walked slowly about the room and discovered a large pile of rags in a corner. He moved closer to the moldy material. As he did, his light reflected from something underneath the pile. Sam stared in horror at Wilson's rolled-back, glassy eyes.

"Oh my gosh!" Sam exclaimed. His hand shook. The quivering light made the corpse's frozen lips look as if they were about to speak. A wave of nausea came over him. Had it not been for the sudden thought that the magnifying glass might still be on the body, he would have run as fast as he could back to the kitchen. He fought down the bile that rose in his throat as he made himself search through Wilson's pockets. But he found nothing.

Moving as quickly away from the body as he could, Sam realized that his socks were sopping wet. Until that moment, he hadn't given any thought to his sneakers that he dropped in the kitchen. Just then, the sound of heavy steps moved across the kitchen floor directly above him. A knot formed in the pit of his stomach, and he froze as the steps moved toward the pantry. It could be Maggie or Otis, but what if it was Malis? What if Malis had somehow made it back to the kitchen and saw his sneakers? He would then know that Sam had hidden there, and that he had followed him. Then a more terrifying thought came to Sam. What if Malis came back down there to search for him? Sam's throat tightened with fear. He couldn't go back up the steps to the pantry, but he was also afraid to go further down the tunnel. He was trapped! But Sam quickly reasoned that if Malis had gone down the passageway and not returned, then there had to be another way out.

With his candle held high, Sam headed in the direction that he had seen Malis go. His mind began to spin with unanswerable questions as he inched his way through the tunnel. Why would Malis kill Wilson? How did he know about the secret passage under Maggie's house? What had happened to the magnifying glass? What if it gets destroyed? Sam knew one thing for certain: the glass brought him there, and only the glass could take him home and likely save his life.

As he moved deeper into the tunnel, he thought about the other passenger on the stagecoach. What had happened to the man in the yellow and black checkered suit? He hadn't seen him since the coach arrived. Maggie had mentioned the room assignments to Wilson, Malis, and Cassy, but she hadn't mentioned another room for the other man. And where was everybody during the fight between Malis and Wilson? How was it that no one else heard the argument or the body being dragged down stairs?

"Oh my gosh," Sam whispered, stopping in his tracks. "What if Malis has killed them all? And Cassy too!" He wondered about Maggie. Had she knowingly let a mass murderer stay at her inn? The more he thought about it, the more frightened he became. Was he next? He had to find out what was happening and why. He had to save Maggie and Cassy if they were still alive. He started to walk faster and faster.

After what seemed like an eternity, Sam came upon a ladder at the end of the tunnel. He set his candle down on the floor. Placing his muddied feet on the slender rungs, he climbed and stretched his arms up until his fingertips touched the splintery roughness of wood. He pushed until the trap door budged. He opened the trap door just enough to recognize the barn floor. Seeing no one, Sam extinguished the candle and climbed out of the tunnel hidden under the granary stairs. Sam gave a sigh of relief as he walked from the barn. He saw Otis help Maggie down from her carriage. She was back! He had to tell her everything. She would know what to do. "Maggie! Maggie!" he shouted, running toward her. "Am I glad to see you!"

Maggie turned from her discussion with Otis, "Boy, what do you mean by screaming at me like a wild man?" She handed him a basket. "Hush, and take this into the house. I'll speak with you in a moment."

Sam started to insist that Maggie hear him out, but Otis stopped him. "Git going, boy," he scolded.

Moving at a snail's pace, Sam looked back to see Otis whispering to Maggie. Sam didn't trust Otis. But by the intent look on Maggie's face, the big man seemed to have something awfully important to say. Maybe Otis knew about Wilson and Malis, and possibly the other people as well. While he waited for Maggie, Sam sat down on the steps of the porch, put down the basket and candle, and slipped off his soggy socks. A shadow moved over him until it totally blocked the sun. Sam felt the color drain from his face as he looked up to see Ephil Malis.

"You should wear your funny clown shoes a little more often," Malis said as he held Sam's sneakers out and dropped them at his feet. "You never know when you might have to run. It isn't safe," Malis hoarsely whispered as he leaned closer, "to go about in stocking feet. You'll catch your death."

Sam's skin prickled. His eyes darted to the nearby door, then back to the rig where Maggie and Otis stood. He tried to call out for her, but when he opened his mouth no sound came out. Malis stood over him, his black gaze pinning the boy to the porch. Only one question filled Sam's mind: did Malis know that he had followed him into the secret passageway and down into the tunnel?

"I can see in the dark, boy," Malis hissed, "and I see what's in people's minds. I know about you." He waved his gnarled hands in front of Sam's face. Suddenly a rope appeared, a rope with a noose at its end.

"Why, Mr. Malis!" Maggie's voice broke Malis' spell. "Doing some more of your magic tricks for the boy?"

Malis straightened and turned to greet Maggie. A smile replaced his evil look, and, in an open display of theatrics, he brought forth a bouquet of flowers from his breast pocket. In addition, with a fancy flourishing of movement, he pulled a lacy handkerchief from the top of Maggie's bonnet.

"Isn't he wonderful, Sam?" Maggie asked, apparently enthralled by the magic trick. "Will there be another show tonight, Mr. Malis?"

Without further hesitation, Sam grabbed his sneakers, jumped to his feet, and ran into the house.

Sam figured that Malis wouldn't hurt Maggie in broad daylight, but then he remembered Cassy. He went straight to her room and rapped quickly on the door.

"Cassy? Cassy, you in there?"

"Where'd I be if I wasn't here?" she answered. "Course I'm here."

Sam heard her start to unlock the door. "NO! Cassy! Don't unlock the door for anyone. Listen. I can't explain. It's a matter of life and death." With his ear pressed against the wood panel, he waited for a reply. "Cassy, did you hear me?"

"I hear ya."

"I'll come get you when it's safe."

Sam knew Cassy would be all right. He ran to his room. He knew he had to try to get Maggie alone so he could tell her about the murder. She had to know everything, and he had to show her the secret passage.

He tried to calm himself as he sat on his bed. He was still afraid, but he felt better for being there. However, unlike Cassy's room, his door didn't have a lock. He began to think that he should have gone into Cassy's room, as he would have been safer there. Malis knew that Sam saw him, and that put Sam in grave danger. He also knew that, despite his fear, he still had to find the magnifying glass.

Sharp footsteps moved down the hall and stopped outside Sam's door. Sweat broke out on Sam's brow as he watched the knob turn. Recalling the look on Malis' face, and how his black eyes seemed to know everything, Sam backed around the bed toward the window.

Long, skinny fingers wrapped around the door's edge as it slowly opened inward. Grasping the window sill, Sam looked down at the ground. Jumping would be his only way out, but better to break an ankle or leg than get caught by Malis.

He straddled the window sill. Just as he was about to jump, Maggie's voice filled the hallway.

"Mr. Malis," she said cheerfully, "can we count on you to be the fourth hand at cards tonight?"

Sam couldn't hear Malis' reply above his own heartbeat, but the door slammed shut.

Heaving a sigh of relief, he swung his leg back through the window. Just when he thought he was safe, the door knob turned again. Sam froze as it slowly opened.

Chapter Five

Sam exhaled with relief as Maggie entered. He started talking as soon as she closed the door. She sat on the bed, a tolerant smile on her face, and listened as she twirled a dust cloth. He told her everything about the magnifying glass, where he had come from, and how he got there. But when he started telling her about Wilson's body, she interrupted, laughing.

"What a wild imagination you have, Sam. You could be a writer. But I'm not sure that a boy your age should be inventin' murder."

"No, Maggie! I'm not making this up!" Then Sam told her about the argument between Wilson and Malis. Maggie's smile faded. When he told her about the secret tunnel beneath the pantry, her expression changed altogether, becoming dark and worrisome.

Rising, she stood with her back toward him, seemingly absorbed in dusting the dresser. "Nonsense," she said stiffly. "If there were such things going on around here, I would know about it."

"You've got to believe me, Maggie!" But by the look on her face, he knew she needed proof. "I'll take you to the tunnel, and you can see for yourself."

"I have no time for such nonsense," she chided as she moved toward the door.

Then Sam blurted, "But what about the other passenger who came off the stagecoach? Where is he now?"

Maggie spun around, her face wrinkled with aggravation. "All right, Sam! What other passenger?"

"You know, the man in the yellow and black checkered suit. I didn't see him come inside, and I didn't see him get back on the coach."

Stunned, Maggie sat back down on the bed. "There was another passenger? I saw only Mr. Malis and Bud."

"And the girl with the black veil," Sam added.

Maggie glared at Sam. "Never mind her. Tell me about the man you saw."

"He was skinny, with a thin mustache, and he wore a yellow and black checkered suit and a derby hat."

"Sounds like a salesman. But if he was a salesman," Maggie uttered, "he would have come in to sell me his wares. Did you notice if he carried a case?'

"No, he didn't have a case."

"Think, Sam, did you see where he went?"

"No, I didn't. The last time I saw him, he'd gone around the side of the coach." He then speculated, "Do you think Ephil Malis killed him too?"

Maggie drooped her shoulders. Sam couldn't tell whether she was frightened or angry. Then it struck him. Maggie didn't seem curious at all about the tunnel, and she didn't even want to go see about the body. He looked at her. The friendliness about her face seemed to vanish. Her gentle features took on a darker, harder look. Her cheerful eyes now looked menacing.

The pieces suddenly fell into place as Sam's mind whirled with fearful realization. Did Maggie know everything? He moved slowly away from her. He realized that she had to be in on it with Malis. She had to be his partner. But that didn't make sense. She would never be Malis' partner or have anything to do with him. Malis was evil; Maggie was not. Then the words that Sam had heard during the argument ran again through his mind: federal marshal … freight … the line … discovered … the station … closed.

Remembering a five-page report that he had done on Harriet Tubman last year in his sixth-grade history class, Sam knew then that he had at least some of the answers. Maggie must be helping Cassy to get to Canada. The inn and the tunnel had to be part of the Underground Railroad. And Maggie was now extremely worried about the missing man in the yellow and black checkered suit. Was he the federal marshal that Wilson and Malis had argued about? That had to be it. Sam looked at Maggie and saw her now in a different light. She and Cassy had to be two of the bravest people he'd ever known. Otis, too, as he had to be part of it. The underground was risky business, as Cassy had described. Maggie knew about the tunnel and Cassy. What she didn't seem to know or believe was that Malis had, for some reason, murdered Wilson.

He had to find out more. He quickly put on his sneakers. As he tied the laces, Ephil Malis' words echoed in his mind, "You never know when you might have to run."

The dust cloth that Maggie had been so nervously twisting slipped to the floor as she looked anxiously out the window.

Sam sat next to her, taking her hands in his. "Maggie, you're the one helping Cassy, aren't you? And you think the skinny man is a federal marshal? That's it, isn't it?"

Maggie started to deny it, but, for some reason, she stopped and simply nodded.

"What does Mr. Malis and Mr. Wilson have to do with all this? And where is Malis now? You gotta tell me, Maggie. He killed Mr. Wilson. I saw it."

Maggie rose suddenly. Before she left the room, she turned and said, "You better go home, Sam. It isn't safe for you around here."

"But Maggie," he said as he followed her out of his room and down the back stairs, "I told you. I can't go without the magnifying glass!"

"I don't have time for such nonsense," she chided him. But she suddenly stopped at the bottom of the stairs as the front door squeaked open. Someone had entered the inn.

"Hush, boy!" she whispered, pushing him into the shadows of the archway. She peeked through the crack of the swinging door that separated the kitchen from the dining room.

"Sam, go back up to your room," her voice quivered with urgency, "and stay there until I come for …"

"You'll be waiting a long time, lad," a strange voice interrupted.

Maggie and Sam spun around. The skinny man in the yellow and black checkered suit stood before them with a gun in one hand and badge in the other. He didn't look at all like what Sam thought a law officer should look like. He looked almost comical. His suit clung too tight, and his pant legs rose above his ankles. The gun looked too big for his hands, and his deep voice sounded as if it came from someone else.

"I'm Ernest P. Tucker, Federal Marshal," he announced as he put his badge back in his pocket. "You can thank your friend Paul Wilson for leading me here. I've been watching this inn long enough to know that it's an active line, and that's against the law." He glanced at Sam. "You in on this too, boy?"

Sam shook his head.

"Then run along home."

Sam paused; he couldn't leave Maggie in such trouble. But before he could react, Otis's big frame rose up behind the marshal and brought a shovel down on his head. Ernest P. Tucker fell unconscious to the floor.

Maggie bent to check the marshal's head. "He'll be all right. Thank goodness you showed up, Otis." She took a rope out from a small cubby-hole under the stairs and handed it to Otis. "Tie him and gag him, then put him in the pantry."

"But Maggie," Sam cried, hardly believing what had happened, "you can't! He's a federal marshal!"

Maggie stopped helping Otis and took Sam aside. "Listen, boy," she said, grabbing his arms, "I have no time to explain. You can untie him in about an hour. We'll be long gone by then. The marshal won't concern himself with you because you're just an innocent boy, aren't you? Now, run as fast as you can up to the barn and get the mare."

As Sam raced across the road, his thoughts fell in order. Once Maggie and Otis got away, he'd tell the marshal about Malis and where to find Wilson's body. The marshal would arrest Malis, and Sam could then go home. But things were happening too fast. With the revelation of the truth about the Underground Railroad, and Maggie and Otis capturing the marshal, Sam had forgotten all about Malis' threats to him. It wasn't until he entered the barn that he became worried again.

Except for the restless bumping of the horses against the sides of their stalls, the barn seemed eerily quiet. Dust hung suspended in the air over the stalls as if frozen in time. Something wasn't right. Sam felt it. He walked past the first stall, past Maggie's horse, and straight to the granary. A cold chill went up his back as he silently crept through the doorway. There, by the trap door, stood Ephil Malis, nervously looking about. Then, with the swiftness of a black snake, he slipped into the tunnel and pulled the trap door down over him. Sam ran to the trap door and stood on top of it. If Malis tried to come back out, he'd have to move Sam first. But as he couldn't remain there all day, Sam looked around for something else to weigh down the hatch. Spying the bales of hay, he quickly maneuvered one into place on top of the trap door.

With this entrance blocked, and too much commotion in the kitchen at the other entrance, Sam hoped that Malis would remain trapped under the house until Sam had time to release the marshal and tell him about Wilson's murder. He studied the bale of hay and worried that it might not hold if Malis pushed with all his might against it. Looking around, Sam saw a tin of nails and a hammer near the stairs. Grabbing them, he frantically hammered ten-penny nails all around the edge of the trapdoor, sealing it permanently shut. Then, to make doubly sure it couldn't be opened, he wedged another bale of hay between the underside of the steps and the tunnel door. Confident that Malis couldn't escape this way, Sam took Maggie's horse and brought her to the front of the inn. All he had to do now was find the magnifying glass, and he'd do that after Maggie and Otis were gone.

As soon as Otis readied the rig, Maggie and Cassy, her face still veiled and gloves in place, exited the inn. As they threw their bags into the wagon, a pair of great blue herons flew overhead. A wide smile spread across Maggie's face as she watched them fly by.

"There's a legend, Sam, that if you stand in the path beneath a great blue heron, happiness and joy will follow you the rest of your life. Let's hope that is true."

Sam smiled. As Cassy climbed into the rig, he leaned close to her. "Good bye, Cassy," he whispered, "I hope you get your land. Someday, all slaves will be free."

"That's a mighty fine thought," she whispered back. He could see her grin through the thick veil.

Before she climbed into the carriage, Maggie took Sam's hands into hers.

"Remember, Sam, wait one hour, then untie the marshal." A look of softness came back to her face as she gazed at him. "Have a good life, boy. I hope you get home all right, wherever home is." She winked at him. Then she climbed into the carriage next to Otis, "Take us away, Mr. Hobbs."

Otis turned and glared down at Sam. The big man still didn't like him. Sam smiled in return. Otis Hobbs. Then Otis looked forward and raised his whip. With a resounding crack of the leather, the horse took off down the road and quickly rounded the bend. Sam waved until they were out of sight. He turned back to the inn. Now alone with Malis, the only protection he had was an unconscious marshal.

Chapter Six

The inn was deathly quiet. Sam expected some noise, as the marshal should be awake and trying to get loose. Sam moved through the parlor and into the dining room on his tiptoes. An ominous feeling overcame him as he pushed the kitchen door open just enough to scan the empty room. He half expected Malis to be there.

Quickly crossing the kitchen, he lifted the latch on the pantry door. His hands shook as he pushed it open. He gasped when he saw that the marshal had escaped his bindings and disappeared. Then Sam noticed the open door to the tunnel.

His whole body quivered with fear. He tried to not panic. Think! Where could the marshal have gone? More importantly, if the trap door is open, where's Malis? What should he do now? He took a deep breath and tried to calm himself. But the pounding of his heart urged him to forget about helping the marshal arrest Malis. He had to find the glass and get back home. But where could he start looking for the glass? Wilson had it at the magic show, so if it wasn't on him, then it had to still be in his room.

Banking on his deductive reasoning being right, Sam climbed the back stairs as quietly as he could. The hall had darkened in the setting sun, and, with Maggie gone, there wasn't anyone to light the lanterns. Malis could be anywhere in the shadows. Sam quickly moved past the first two rooms, but their opened doors revealed nothing out of the ordinary. As he crept toward the magician's room, he forgot about the loose board alongside the door and stepped right on it. The morgue-like silence of the hall intensified the creak until it sounded like the whole house was falling down.

Sam stood frozen against the wall. If Ephil Malis had heard the creak, then he would know exactly where to find Sam. He listened for footsteps, but he heard no other sound except for his own erratic breathing. With caution, he slipped into Wilson's room and started his search. He looked beneath the bed, checked under the dresser, and rifled through the drawers. The magnifying glass wasn't anywhere in the room.

The door slammed behind him. Terror seized Sam as he spun around. "Malis!"

The murderer stood in front of the door with only the narrow bed separating them.

"We have unfinished business, boy," Malis snarled, "and this time Mistress Hall isn't here to save you. Oh, yes," he said as a smirk stretched across his thin lips, "I saw her and Otis leave. By the time they get back, you'll be where all snoopers end up – in the grave!"

Sam could only think of one way to save himself; he had to try to bluff his way out. Malis couldn't know that Maggie had left for good. Sam's mind whirled with a glimmer of hope. If he could bluff Malis into thinking that they were coming back soon, then Malis might take him to the barn to stay out of Maggie's sight. Then, while going from the inn to the barn, they were bound to run across the marshal. He had to be out there somewhere. It was worth a try … and the only one Sam had.

"Otis only took Maggie down the road," Sam said, trying to sound nonchalant, "they'll be back any minute."

"Any minute? Where'd they go?" Malis demanded as he looked toward the window.

Sam couldn't think fast enough for an answer as he stammered, "To … to …"

Malis didn't seem fooled. He suddenly lunged across the bed and grabbed at Sam. Sam pulled back and darted around the bed for the door, but Malis got there first.

Seizing the boy with a steel grip, the murderer dragged him, squirming and kicking, down the back stairs. Frantic with fear, Sam realized that Malis was taking him to the pantry and not outside. How would the marshal find him now? How would he escape from the tunnel? Sam fought harder to get free. But no matter how hard he squirmed, hit, and kicked, Malis succeeded in dragging his prisoner through the trap door and down the steps.

Light filled the passageway from the secret room. Shadows, like crouching trolls, leapt up the walls as Malis pulled Sam into the room and slammed him down on the chair. As the shadows shrank, Wilson's body came into view. Reflecting candle light danced off his glassy eyes and made them seem as if they followed Malis' every move. Sam shuddered under their grotesque stare. He still shook as Malis took a piece of rope from a support beam and tied him to the chair.

"You won't get away with this," Sam cried as he squirmed to get free.

"Of course I will," snarled Malis as he yanked the ropes tighter. "I already have."

Then, turning up the light, he directed his attention to a row of cylinder-shaped objects on the table.

"The marshal will stop you!" Sam yelled, hoping that he would be heard upstairs.

Malis spun around and stopped. "What did you say? What marshal?" He grabbed Sam by his collar.

"The one who came here to arrest Maggie and Otis." Sam realized his mistake before he even finished speaking.

"So," Malis released him. His sneer turned into a sick smile, "they aren't coming back as you would have me believe. They've absconded and left you holding the bag. My good fortune." He tightened the ropes around Sam.

Sam cringed as stout cord cut into his arms. "What are you going to do with me?" His voice quivered.

"I can't very well let you live, now can I? Seeing as you know of my little indiscretion over there." Malis glanced toward Wilson's body.

"But I didn't see you kill him!"

"Be that as it may, you know I did."

Malis again looked at Wilson's body. "Stupid fool," he said, directing his words to the corpse, "you thought I smuggled slaves because I believed in your silly cause. It was for the money. Abolitionist sympathizers paid plenty for my help to bring them here, and the slave hunters paid just as much to have them returned. Who noticed or cared if some of the slaves didn't reach the border? Then we got paid twice, didn't we? Too bad your conscience got to you, and you contacted the marshal's office. What did it get you? Now this line is ruined. Stupid fool!" Malis walked over to Wilson's corpse and kicked it. A bloated hand slipped from beneath the rags and fell on the dirt with a dull thud. Sam felt sick.

Malis turned back to Sam. "It was a lofty, philanthropic cause with Mistress Hall. She never cared about the money, only the people. Foolish woman! But I deserve the money, as I took all the risks to make each connection." He thumped his chest angrily. "I had to do all the dirty work myself, and so I deserve all the money." Malis moved into the darkness, and then he returned with a small wooden keg which he placed on the table. He took a cigar from his jacket pocket, lit it, and inhaled deeply. Sam coughed as the exhaled smoke curled around his head. Malis took a few more puffs, then remarked, "Oh, I must be careful now, mustn't I?" He placed the cigar on the far edge of the table and began to empty the contents of the keg into the tubes. As Malis worked, Sam read the bold, black lettering on the keg: GUNPOWDER.

"What … what are you going to do?" Sam asked, nervously.

With a sinister smile, Malis showed him one of the tubes. Wound at both ends like a giant Tootsie Roll, Sam realized that Malis was making bombs.

"Oh my gosh," Sam cried as he tried again to break free, "what are you going to do with those?"

"You mean you haven't figured it out yet?" Malis put the tube on the table and began to fill another one. "Gunpowder is used for other things besides smoke screens on a barnyard stage. It's used for blowing up things, and," he looked intently at Sam, "for burying witnesses."

Filled with desperation, Sam violently struggled to free himself. He had to stall for time. The marshal had to be somewhere. But did he even know about the tunnel? And what about the magnifying glass? If Sam got loose, could he even find it?

In an attempt to stall Malis, Sam demanded to know, "What about Mr. Wilson's magic glass? What did you do with it?"

"You mean this?" Pulling the magnifying glass from his coat pocket, Malis held it in front of Sam. "It's evidence. I'm going to dispose of it along with the other evidence that could get me hung, which would be Wilson and you."

Sam's stomach churned. The sickening realization that Malis fully intended to kill him firmly set in. He had to buy more time; he needed to keep Malis talking in the hopes that the marshal would eventually stumble on the passageway and the tunnel. Suddenly, what Malis had said about the magnifying glass as being evidence sunk in. "You used that glass to kill Mr. Wilson?"

Malis snickered. "It wasn't the best choice of weapons, as it wasn't big enough to completely do the job, but it did sufficiently stun him so that I could strangle him." He pushed his face into Sam's. "What's your interest in this glass, anyhow? Hold on a minute! When Otis brought it to me, he said something about a boy stealing it. You're that boy. Now you want it back. Why?"

Sam tried to think fast. "Umm … it's worth a lot of money. I was going to sell it, that's all."

"You're not going to need money where you're going." Malis placed the magnifying glass next to the keg and filled the last tube with gunpowder. Once finished, he shoved half the tubes into his coat pockets. Then taking one of the tubes, he tucked a small cord into one end and placed it across the other tubes stacked beside the keg.

"And now, we part," he said as he reached for his cigar and lit the fuse, "leaving the authorities a pile of rubble and a mystery."

The damp fuse smoldered slowly as Malis' evil laughter faded from the room. The newspaper had stated that there were two skeletons found in the rubble of the inn. One was Paul Wilson. The other … was him! Frantically, Sam bounced the chair in an attempt to break it. The fuse burned faster. The chair didn't break.

The ropes stretched with all his moving about, but not enough to get his hands free. Just as he was about to give up hope, Sam heard scuffling in the passageway. He bounced the chair around to face the door and held his breath. Relief washed over him when he saw the marshal. But the sizzling of the fuse urged him into action. The marshal seemed dazed as he leaned against the doorway.

"Hurry!" Sam yelled. "The fuse! It's gonna blow!"

"What are you talking about?" The marshal then saw the tiny red glow of the fuse. He raced over and pulled the fuse free. He stamped it out with his foot.

Once freed, Sam snatched the magnifying glass from the table, grabbed the marshal's arm, and pulled him from the room. "Hurry," he cried, "Malis has more gunpowder in his pockets!"

The glow of a second fuse caught his attention on the floor just outside the room. Another lit bomb rolled towards them from the direction of the barn exit.

Without hesitation, they sprinted to the pantry steps and up through the opening into the kitchen. The trap door clicked shut behind them. They didn't stop running until they reached the barn. From that safe distance, Sam looked back.

Just as the marshal opened his mouth to speak, the earth shook in repeated episodes of increasing intensity. The final explosion knocked them to the ground. A tremendous plume of smoke rose from the inn as flames quickly spread from the kitchen to the rest of the Blue Heron Inn.

"Jumping Jehoshaphat!" the marshal cried as he stood. "That was close."

"But where's Malis?" asked Sam as he struggled to his feet.

The marshal related how he had come upon the trapdoor in the pantry and snuck down the steps just as Malis revealed his plans to Sam. "I wanted to lay in wait by the doorway and catch him by surprise, but he came out of the room sooner than I expected. He ran smack dab into me and knocked the wind out of both of us. He ran down into the tunnel before I could catch my breath."

Sam gasped. "Down into the tunnel? But he couldn't get out that way; I nailed the door shut at the other end."

Scratching his head, Tucker added, "Unless there was another way out, I guess he would've tried to come back to the pantry to get out. I don't think he even got that far. I know one thing, if he didn't die in that explosion, he'll be hung for sure when I find him."

Sam held the magnifying glass behind his back as he looked at the flaming building. He knew then that Malis had to be the second skeleton.

"Well, boy, not much more can be done around here. Your friends must be well on their way to Canada by now. I really didn't have the heart to arrest them anyhow. I'll be glad when I can get back to catching actual criminals." He looked down at Sam. "Where's your folks? Far from here?"

"No. Just across the field. But first I have to get my … my jacket. I left it in the granary. If I come home without it, my mom will skin me alive." Sam didn't want to lie, but he had to have a good reason to go into the barn.

"Run along, then," the marshal said with a knowing smile as if he knew how mothers were.

Sam ran up the earthen ramp and into the barn. Gripping the magnifying glass so tightly that his hand hurt, he slowly moved toward the granary. What if it didn't work? What if the magic had left it? What if the glass wasn't what brought him into that time after all? He guessed he could live in that time period without too much adjustment, and he did have the advantage of knowing most of what would transpire in the country since 1860 thanks to his history classes. Still, he paused to say a prayer that the magnifying glass held just enough magical power to get him back to where he belonged. Shaking, he stood before the mirror and slowly raised the glass to his eye.

"Hey, son," the marshal called from the barn entrance, "I don't see no house across the field. Where did you say you lived?" He walked back to the granary. "Boy, where'd you get to?"

The magical force once again knocked Sam to the ground. Only this time he knew it wasn't an earthquake or an explosion. He sat with his eyes closed, afraid to get up, afraid to see what period of time he was in. The droning of a bee close to his ear made him open his eyes. With inexpressible relief and joy, he saw that the barn once again looked old and dusty. Scrambling to his feet, Sam looked excitedly out the window. He saw the tool shed with his ten-speed bike, and, beyond that, his house! His grandfather's house! He was home!

The trowel still lay on the floor where he had dropped it. Sam wrapped an old rag around the magnifying glass and pushed it firmly back into the ground where he had found it. He then replaced the board and sat staring at it. He wondered if Malis had buried it there instead of leaving it next to the gunpowder. Sam then wondered who could have trapped Malis in the tunnel since Sam couldn't actually have been the one to do it. Sam recalled that Maggie's hired boy had disappeared. Did he take that boy's place? Sam shook his head. It was all too confusing for him to figure out. Whatever happened, there were two bodies found in the ruins of the inn, and somebody had buried the magnifying glass, right where he found it.

Sam moved to the decaying stairs across the room. Years of dust covered the floor, hiding the seams of the trapdoor. As Sam stared down at it, he knew he'd have to pry the door open or he'd always wonder what, if anything, lay beneath it. The boards came up easily with the help of the trowel. The explosion had completely reached that side of the tunnel, for dirt and debris packed the opening. The force pushed a rung from the ladder against the back of the trapdoor. Sam closed the trapdoor and pushed the rusted nails back into their rotted slots.

As he headed toward the house, Sam wondered how he would explain where he had been since the day before. Then he saw his favorite shirt on the laundry line, and he quickly realized that this had to be the same load of clothes that his mother had hung right before he left. She would never leave her laundry out overnight. Time had only moved for him and for those at the Blue Heron Inn. He then looked down at the shirt he wore. Dirt covered most of it. It had a tear on one side and a bright red stain on the front. Fortunately, his mother wouldn't miss that old shirt. He wouldn't need to explain its condition, except for maybe the red stain. He looked closer at the stain. It wasn't blood. He smiled as he realized what it had to be. "At least I've got proof of my adventure, a 19th century blob of Maggie's strawberry rhubarb pie."

A lone blue heron suddenly flew overhead and came to earth by the stream on Mr. Brook's property. As Sam stood still and watched it, he felt older and wiser. He remembered what Maggie had said about the great blue heron, and he wondered if one day he'd ever find out what happened to her and Cassy. But one thing he did know for sure as he ran into his house beneath the path of the blue heron: happiness and joy had followed him home, just as Maggie had predicted.

About the Authors

Rachel Secor is the pseudonym for the mother and daughter writing team of Leona Callander Seaver and Belinda Barrett. They've collaborated on numerous writing projects over the years, and they even attended college together at one point: Leona focused on history, and Belinda obtained a BA and MA in English literature. When not writing, they spend time seeking family connections in genealogy; Rachel Secor is one of their ancestors. The authors live in upstate New York.

www.ingramcontent.com/pod-product-compliance
Lightning Source LLC
Chambersburg PA
CBHW020615310726
48979CB00008B/1495/J

* 9 7 8 1 9 3 9 0 9 8 0 6 1 *